P9-DBI-873

THE AMERICAN GIRLS

17  64

KAYA, an adventurous Nez Perce girl whose deep love
for horses and respect for nature nourish her spirit

17  74

FELICITY, a spunky, spritely colonial girl,
full of energy and independence

18  24

JOSEFINA, an Hispanic girl whose heart and
hopes are as big as the New Mexico sky

18  54

KIRSTEN, a pioneer girl of strength and
spirit who settles on the frontier

18  64

ADDY, a courageous girl determined to be
free in the midst of the Civil War

19  04

SAMANTHA, a bright Victorian beauty, an
orphan raised by her wealthy grandmother

19  34

KIT, a clever, resourceful girl facing the
Great Depression with spirit and determination

19  44

MOLLY, who schemes and dreams on the
home front during World War Two

1764

KAYA'S HERO

A Story of Giving

BY JANET SHAW

ILLUSTRATIONS BILL FARNSWORTH

VIGNETTES SUSAN McALINEY

American Girl®

Visit our Web site at **americangirl.com**

Printed in China.
02 03 04 05 06 07 08 LEO 12 11 10 9 8 7 6 5 4 3 2 1

The American Girls Collection®, Kaya™, and American Girl®
are trademarks of Pleasant Company.

PICTURE CREDITS
The following individuals and organizations have generously given
permission to reprint images contained in "Looking Back":

pp. 66–67—Photo by Marc Lemereaux, courtesy of National Park Service, Nez Perce National
Park (parfleche); Photo by Marc Lemereaux, courtesy of National Park Service, Nez Perce
National Historical Park (arrows/rope); Dakota Quillwork Sewing Kit, Glenbow Collection,
Calgary, Alberta, Canada (AF 2389) (buffalo bladder); Photo by Marc Lemereaux, courtesy of
National Park Service, Nez Perce National Historical Park (beaded dress); pp. 68–69—Photo by
Roy Zipstein (portrait of Elissia Powaukee); Northwest Museum of Arts and Culture/Eastern
Washington State Historical Society, Spokane, WA (snowshoes); pp. 70–71—Photo courtesy of
National Park Service, Nez Perce National Historical Park, NEPE-HI-2448 (elder woman).

Library of Congress Cataloging-in-Publication Data

Shaw, Janet Beeler, 1937–
Kaya's hero : a story of giving / by Janet Shaw ;
illustrations, Bill Farnsworth ; vignettes, Susan McAliley.

p. cm. — (The American girls collection)

Summary: In 1764, Kaya greatly admires a courageous and kind
young woman in her Nez Perce village and wants to be worthy of
her respect. Includes historical notes on the winter activities of the
Nez Perce Indians, including ceremonies and crafts.
ISBN 1-58485-428-6 — ISBN 1-58485-427-8 (pbk.)
[1. Self-esteem—Fiction. 2. Conduct of life—Fiction. 3. Nez Perce
Indians—Fiction. 4. Indians of North America—Northwest,
Pacific—Fiction. 5. Northwest, Pacific—Fiction.] I. Farnsworth,
Bill, ill. II. McAliley, Susan, ill. III. Title.

PZ7.S534228 Kay 2002 [Fic]—dc21 2001036811

FOR MY SON, MARK,
HIS WIFE, SUE,
AND THEIR BOYS, SAM AND MAX,
WITH LOVE

Kaya and her family are
Nimíipuu, known today
as Nez Perce Indians.
They speak the Nez Perce
language, so you'll see
some Nez Perce words in
this book. Kaya is short
for the Nez Perce name
Kaya'aton'my', which means
"she who arranges rocks."
You'll find the meanings
and pronunciations of
these and other Nez Perce
words in the glossary on
page 72.

TABLE OF CONTENTS

KAYA'S FAMILY
AND FRIENDS

KAYA'S FAMILY

TOE-TA
Kaya's father, an expert horseman and wise village leader.

EETSA
Kaya's mother, who is a good provider for her family and her village.

KAYA
An adventurous girl with a generous spirit.

WING FEATHER AND SPARROW
Kaya's mischievous twin brothers.

BROWN DEER
Kaya's sister, who is old enough to court.

PI-LAH-KA
AND KAUTSA
*Eetsa's parents, who
guide and comfort Kaya.*

TWO HAWKS
*A Salish boy who
becomes Kaya's friend.*

SWAN CIRCLING
*A strong warrior woman
whom Kaya admires.*

RUNAWAY HORSE!

Kaya knelt on a mat in the winter lodge
and leaned over the baby named Light
On The Water, who lay in her *tee-kas.*
"Tawts may-we!" Kaya crooned to her. "Are you
unhappy this morning?"

Light On The Water gazed steadily into Kaya's
eyes, but her mouth trembled and turned down as if
she was about to cry.

Kaya stroked the plump, warm cheek. "Are you
wet? Is that what you're telling me?" she asked. She
loosened the lacing of the buckskin that wrapped the
baby and pulled it away from her feet and legs. The
soft cattail fluff that cushioned the baby's bottom
was soaked. Kaya pulled it out, dried the baby, and

1

placed fresh fluff underneath her. She squeezed one of the baby's little toes and kissed her forehead. Light On The Water smiled now. *"Tawts!"* Kaya said as she laced up the covering again.

Running Alone, Kaya's young aunt, put her hand on Kaya's shoulder. "Won't you make the lacing just a little tighter?" she asked. "We're going to ride out to gather wood for the fires, and I want my baby very safe."

Kaya tightened the lacing, then carried the baby out of the lodge. The day was chilly, and Light On The Water's breath was a small cloud at her lips. When Running Alone had mounted her horse, Kaya handed her the baby. Running Alone slipped the carrying strap of the *tee-kas* over her saddle horn and gazed down at her smiling daughter. "She likes your gentle touch," she told Kaya.

"She's so easy to care for," Kaya said. "Not like my little brothers. Look, they think I can't see them hiding behind that tree." She pointed at the two sets of dark eyes gleaming through the branches of a pine. "Boys, let's go riding!" she called to the twins, and they came running, clutching robes of spotted fawn skin around their shoulders. Like all *Nimíipuu* children, they loved to be on horseback.

Kaya helped one twin climb up behind her older sister, Brown Deer. Then Kaya mounted a chestnut mare and lifted up the other twin. As she waited for the other women and children to mount, she glanced up toward the north. The foothills of the distant mountains were already white-robed with snow, but here in Salmon River Country the earth was still brown and bare. Each winter, Kaya's band came to these sheltering hills to make their winter village. They put up their lodges near the banks of the stream and stayed until spring, when it was time to move up to the prairie to dig nourishing roots and bulbs for food.

Kaya pulled her elk robe more tightly around her shoulders. Even dressed warmly in fur-lined moccasins, leggings, and her robe, Kaya shivered in the chill of winter. But she remembered the heat of late summer, when enemies from Buffalo Country made a raid on her people to steal horses. Kaya's horse, Steps High, was stolen with other Nimíipuu horses. And in the raid Kaya and her sister, Speaking Rain, were captured as slaves and taken far away to the enemy camp. There they met a

Salish boy, Two Hawks, who was also held as a slave. Kaya and Two Hawks had managed to escape and cross the mountains back to her people. But Speaking Rain, who was blind, had insisted that she couldn't keep up—that Kaya must leave her behind.

Kaya shivered again. She remembered, too, how cold—and hungry!—she and Two Hawks had been as they made their way over the Buffalo Trail. Now she and the boy were safe again, fed by the meat and warmed by the hides of animals that had given themselves to her people. But Two Hawks had broken his ankle on the trail, and it was slow to heal. He sat alone and homesick all day.

Kaya felt as if she had two aches in her chest. One ache was a sharp-edged gratitude that she was with her family again. But the other was a stab of grief that Speaking Rain was still a captive. Kaya had promised that they would be together again, but where was her sister now? If Kaya could find her, how could she save her? And would she ever see her beautiful, beloved horse again?

Soon Kaya was riding single file with the others. After a time, they came to a bowl-shaped canyon where trees grew thickly. The children ran to play, and the women fanned out along the creek to gather wood. A girl named Little Fawn and some boys were climbing aspen saplings and swinging to and fro on them.

"Magpie, fly into the trees with us!" Little Fawn called to Kaya.

Magpie! Kaya winced. She tried to ignore that awful nickname the children had given her when they were all switched for her offense.

"Not now!" she called back. "I'm going to look for more fluff for the baby."

She glanced toward Light On The Water and Running Alone, who was tethering her horse to a tree. The baby, lulled by the rocking ride, napped in her tee-kas on the saddle horn. Taking a twined bag, Kaya started for the stream after the other women.

Suddenly, a sharp crack echoed across the canyon. Kaya whirled around—the branch Little Fawn was pulling on had broken off. Little Fawn jumped to the ground. The branch slashed down like a spear and struck the rump of Running Alone's horse. The startled horse reared up in alarm and broke her tether. Wild-eyed, the panicked horse began to bolt down the canyon, the baby in the

5

tee-kas still hanging on the saddle!

"Stop! Stop!" Running Alone cried out. She ran after the galloping horse.

Kaya ran, too. The fleeing horse was already halfway down the canyon and heading for the narrow opening and open country beyond. The tee-kas bumped against the horse's shoulder with each plunging step. Would the baby be tossed off? Light On The Water could be hurt badly—or killed!

Near the canyon opening, the young woman named Swan Circling came rushing from the woods. Dropping her robe behind her, she ran swiftly to cut off the horse's escape. She reached the opening of the canyon first and spun around to face the galloping horse, which was thundering straight at her. Taking a stand, she spread her arms wide, like an eagle in flight.

Would the horse run her down? Swan Circling stood her ground. Right in front of her, the runaway skidded to a halt. The horse snorted and tossed her head, flinging lather onto both Swan Circling and the baby.

Swan Circling seized the horse's reins. She held the horse firmly in place as Running Alone came

*Swan Circling spun around to face the galloping horse,
which was thundering straight at her.*

rushing to get her baby.

Running Alone lifted the tee-kas from the saddle horn and clutched it to her chest. "My little one!" she cried, kissing her baby's face over and over. "You saved my baby, Swan Circling! *Katsee-yow-yow!* I can never thank you enough!"

Kaya came running right behind her aunt. She reached to take hold of the reins, too, and stroked the horse's neck and shoulder to calm her.

"I saw you step in front of my horse, but how did you get her to halt?" Running Alone asked. "She could have run right past you—or right over you!"

"I didn't think of that," Swan Circling said. "I wanted her to stop, and she did. Is your baby all right?"

Light On The Water was grinning. She thought the bouncing, runaway ride was a game.

Swan Circling glanced at Kaya, who was still stroking the horse's lathered neck. "You seem to have a way with horses," she said approvingly. "She's quieting down. Will you lead her back now?"

Kaya held the reins of the uneasy horse securely as she and Swan Circling returned to the others. As they walked, she studied Swan Circling's calm face.

Kaya had been curious about Swan Circling ever since she'd married Claw Necklace and joined the band. And now Kaya remembered that the woman who appeared to her when she was lost on the Buffalo Trail had looked like Swan Circling. Had that vision been a sign that they would be friends? Kaya hoped so. She wished she could become as strong as this brave young woman who hadn't even flinched when a horse charged straight at her!

Later that day, Kaya sat with other girls and women at one end of a lodge that several families shared. Many layers of tule mats and hides covered the lodge. Parfleches and piles of hide blankets were stacked along the bottom to keep out drafts. The women unfolded the hides they'd tanned in the summer and set about making moccasins and clothes and carrying cases. They took out the hemp cord they'd twisted and wove baskets and bags. They made their clothes beautiful with fringe and beads and quill decorations. Kaya loved working with the others in the warm winter lodge.

Kaya watched Brown Deer stringing a necklace of beads made from shells. From time to time, Brown Deer ran her fingers lovingly across the beads. The necklace was for a man—and Kaya guessed her sister was making it for Cut Cheek. The two had danced together last summer, and soon they'd see each other again when he came with other neighboring villagers for the winter gatherings. Each day now, Brown Deer combed her hair and dressed it with fragrant oil so it would grow long and silky.

Kaya's mother, *Eetsa*, was finishing a large twined storage bag, one of the many, many gifts they would give to family and friends when they came to visit.

Kautsa, Kaya's grandmother, was weaving a small hat. Kaya watched her grandmother's expert work closely—because the hat was for her. Kaya would wear it in the spring when she went to dig roots with the other girls and women. She loved the zigzags of red beargrass that Kautsa worked into the design.

Kaya put aside the basket she was weaving and picked up her sister's worn buckskin doll. Speaking Rain had carried her doll everywhere she went. With

her sister gone, Kaya kept the doll close to her.
As she adjusted the doll's dress, she discovered
a tear in her back, a bit of deer-hair stuffing
poking out. She decided to mend it and
have it ready for Speaking Rain when she
was with them again.

Kaya wanted to care for the doll because she
feared she hadn't taken good care of Speaking Rain.
When the enemies had made their raid in the night
last summer, Eetsa had told Kaya to take Speaking
Rain to hide in the woods. But Kaya went first to
look for her horse—and enemies seized her and her
sister and carried them off. How Kaya regretted that
she hadn't done as her mother told her! *If I were as
strong as Swan Circling,* Kaya thought, *I'd find a way
to get my sister back.*

"Kautsa, may I ask you a question?" Kaya asked
quietly.

"*Aa-heh,* you may ask me anything," Kautsa said.
A slight smile crinkled the corners of her eyes. "Ask—
then I'll decide if I want to answer you."

"You're teasing," Brown Deer said, laughing.
"You always answer us!"

"It's true," Kautsa said. "I've always answered

11

your questions—so far! What do you want to know?"

Kaya threaded her bone needle with a bit of sinew and began stitching the tear in the buckskin doll. "I want to ask about Swan Circling. What makes her so—different?"

"Different?" Kautsa said. "You must be asking me how Swan Circling came to be a warrior woman. Now, there's a story!"

"Can you tell us?" Brown Deer asked eagerly.

Kautsa nodded. Her fingers were busy as she twined the brown hemp with the yellow beargrass. "Swan Circling came to live with us when she and

Claw Necklace married, three winters ago. We all saw right away that she was a strong girl, eager to help. Then . . ." Kautsa paused and held the hat she was weaving above Kaya's head to check the size. The many strands of cord trailing from the hat tickled Kaya's nose.

"Then?" Kaya prompted her grandmother.

"Then?" Brown Deer echoed. "What happened then, Kautsa?"

Kautsa put the hat back into her lap and began to work on it again. "Then Swan Circling went with her husband on a hunting trip to Buffalo Country. While they slept one night, enemies attacked them!"

"To steal horses, as they did with us?" Kaya asked.

"Not to steal horses," Kautsa said. "They came to fight—or to show their courage just by touching our warriors! Our men rushed from the tepees to defend themselves. Claw Necklace hurried into the skirmish. But in his eagerness to fight, he left behind his bow and arrows."

"He didn't have any weapons?" Kaya asked.

"Ah-heh, he was in great danger!" Kautsa said.

13

"Instead of running for cover with the other women, Swan Circling picked up his weapons and ran after him into the fight. Arrows flew around her. One even singed her arm, but it didn't pierce her flesh. She gave her husband the bow and arrows so he could fight well, and then she tended our wounded men. She was never wounded by arrows, though a few tore her dress."

"Did Swan Circling tell you this?" Kaya asked.

"She would never speak of her bravery," Kautsa said. "It was Claw Necklace who told us what had happened. After our men won the fight, they gave Swan Circling an eagle feather for her bravery—a very high honor, as you know."

"I know she goes to battles," Brown Deer said. "She brings fresh horses to the riders whose horses have been hurt."

"So she does," Kautsa said. "Swan Circling has brought many things to us. You were with her when she saved Running Alone's baby, weren't you, Kaya?"

"Aa-heh, Kautsa," Kaya said. "I saw it all."

"Then you know she's fearless," Kautsa said. "I believe she wouldn't hesitate to fight a grizzly bear! There's only one sad thing—"

Brown Deer stopped stringing beads and looked up. "What sad thing?" Brown Deer asked.

"As you know, Swan Circling doesn't have any children. That's sad, don't you think?" Kautsa asked.

"It would be very sad not to have any children," Brown Deer said slowly, as if she were imagining how she'd feel if she were Swan Circling.

"But she and her husband are young," Eetsa broke in. "There's still plenty of time for them to have children."

"Aa-heh," Kautsa agreed. "There's time for children. And they'll be strong, like her, I'm sure of that." Then she tapped Kaya's hand. "I'm glad you mended your sister's doll, Granddaughter."

Eetsa rose to her knees and peered into the cooking basket. "We need some water so we can cook our meal," she announced.

Right away Kaya got to her feet to go fetch the water. She caught up with Little Fawn on the trail to the stream. Like Kaya, Little Fawn carried a large water basket, but she was limping. "Did you hurt yourself when the branch broke?" Kaya asked. "Maybe you climbed too high."

Little Fawn winced at each step, but she shook her head. "It's nothing. I've jumped out of trees much higher than that."

Other women and girls were drawing water at the stream. Kaya saw Swan Circling a little way downstream, leading a spotted mare. As the mare drank, Swan Circling dampened a bundle of leaves and tied it onto the mare's back. Kaya went downstream to her side. She'd been eager to see Swan Circling again, but now that she stood beside her, she didn't know what to say. She stroked the mare's flank. "This is a pretty one," she said. "Has she got sores on her back?"

"Aa-heh," Swan Circling said. "The men saw her rolling in a patch of sage to heal herself. They asked me to make a poultice of the sage for her."

"The spots on her rump remind me of my horse, Steps—" Kaya stopped, afraid to go on for fear her voice would break.

Swan Circling glanced at her with concern in her eyes. "You miss your horse, don't you," she said. "I just saw the boy who escaped with you."

Kaya leaned out and dipped her water basket into the stream. "Two Hawks can't put weight on his broken ankle yet," she said. "He has to be patient."

"You're right," Swan Circling said. "It takes time for bone to heal. But he looks lonesome and grumpy."

"That's because he doesn't like to be patient!" Kaya said.

Swan Circling laughed. "That's the kind of boy he is! It's good you were with him when you escaped. You're a dependable girl, I can see that. You two were very strong to run away and find your way back. It's too bad he's unhappy here with us."

Kaya's cheeks burned with pleasure at this praise from the woman she admired so much. To keep Swan Circling from seeing that she was blushing, Kaya turned her head.

Little Fawn was standing on the shore a little way upstream, a basket of water in her arms. When Kaya looked her way, Little Fawn lifted her chin and narrowed her eyes. "Magpie flew back to her nest!" she said, and limped away. Was she jealous of the praise Kaya had been given?

"Magpie?" Swan Circling said. "Is that your nickname, Kaya?" She patted the mare's rump and took her lead rope.

"They call me that sometimes," Kaya said.

Swan Circling gave Kaya a searching look. "Some nicknames dig into us like bear claws," she said. "As you grow older, they don't hurt so much. Will you remember that, Kaya?"

"Aa-heh," Kaya said. "I'll remember."

"Tawts!" Swan Circling said with approval. She started to lead the mare back to the men who tended the horses.

Kaya bit her lip as she watched Swan Circling walking back to the herd. Swan Circling had offered her good advice about her nickname. But, of course, she didn't know that Kaya had gotten it last summer because she'd gone off to race her horse instead of taking care of her brothers. Whipwoman had scolded Kaya, saying she must learn to think of others before she thought of herself. If Swan Circling knew that, she'd certainly regret calling Kaya strong—or dependable. And if she knew it was Kaya's fault that she and Speaking Rain had been taken captive, would Swan Circling have any respect for her at all?

C H A P T E R
T W O

LESSONS FROM A BASKET

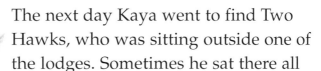

The next day Kaya went to find Two Hawks, who was sitting outside one of the lodges. Sometimes he sat there all day without moving, an antelope hide wrapped tightly around him. "I know you can't walk yet, but I bet you can ride," Kaya said to him.

Two Hawks frowned—he understood only a few words of her language.

Kaya used her hands to speak to him. *Do you want to ride with me?*

"*Wah-tu!*" he said. He'd learned the word for "no" right away. He shrugged, his lips turned down. With his hands he signed, *Leave me alone!*

But Kaya wasn't going to leave him alone. She'd

been thinking about what Swan Circling had said—
Two Hawks was unhappy. Kaya's father had
promised they would help Two Hawks get back to
his people in the spring, but that time was a long
way off. Since Two Hawks had been here, he hadn't
smiled once. Kaya couldn't help him get home any
faster, but she could be a better friend to him.

She signed to him, *You can't just sit there. I'm
going to get a horse for you.*

"*Wah-tu!*" he said again and shook his head.

But the word "no" was a challenge to Kaya. She
went to get the chestnut horse she rode and another
gentle mare. She put light rope bits on them and led
them back to where Two Hawks sat, his chin on his
knees. "Two Hawks!" she called to him. She threw
him the words, *Let's go! Let's ride!*

He shook his head angrily. *I can't ride,* he signed.
My ankle is broken. He pointed to the splint that was
bound to his ankle.

You can do it! she signed. *I'll help you,* she added,
though she wasn't sure how she could get him onto
the horse.

Two Hawks grimaced as if he was determined
to prove her wrong. He pushed to one foot,

20

supporting himself with a crutch made from a cottonwood branch. Kaya led the gentle mare close to him. Two Hawks looked at Kaya darkly, as if to say, "What now?"

She thought a moment. Then she signed to him, *Put your knee in my hands. I can lift you onto the horse.*

Two Hawks looked at the horse, then back at her. He shook his head. Did this stubborn boy think she wasn't strong enough to lift him? She clasped her hands and held them by his injured leg. After a moment, he gingerly placed his knee in her grip and grabbed the horse's mane with both hands. "Now!" Kaya said. She lifted, he threw his good leg over the horse's back, and he was mounted.

Kaya studied him. He wasn't grimacing with pain. In fact, he looked pleased. She climbed onto her horse and beckoned for him to come with her. She'd thought of something Two Hawks could do while his leg healed. She threw him the words, *We have to find an elderberry stick so you can make a flute.*

Overnight it had grown colder. A sharp wind whined around the lodge where Kaya and other

21

children were dressing themselves after their morning swim. But the lodge was warmed by five fires lined up down the center, smoke rising through the long opening at the top. Eetsa and the other women were already cooking a morning meal because there was much work to do that day.

Kaya knew that soon friends and family would come from other villages nearby for the new year celebration, when the short winter days begin to grow longer again. People would share their news and give each other gifts. They'd feast and tell stories and honor *Hun-ya-wat,* who made the seasons and held them in balance.

Today the women were putting up another lodge, one large enough to hold everyone for the feasts. When Kaya joined them, she saw Swan Circling helping to raise one of the long lodge poles and set it onto the frame of tepee poles. Kaya thought the framework looked like the backbone and ribs of a skeleton of a huge horse. After the women completed the frame, they would cover it with tule mats and hides. Kaya helped other girls carry the rolled-up mats and place them near the builders. She kept Swan Circling in sight, hoping to have a chance to talk with her again.

With the lodge finished, Kaya followed Swan
Circling to another lodge where women were
preparing more food so that there would be enough
for the visitors. Eetsa and Running Alone were
making pemmican, a mixture of dried meat
and berries. With a stone pestle, they
were pounding dried deer meat in one of
the large mortars. When one of them got
tired using the heavy stone pestle, they
traded places. Kaya thought the steady *thump,
thump, thump* sounded like a heartbeat.

Swan Circling joined the women, and Kaya
went to peek at Light On The Water, who was snug
in her tee-kas.

"Would you give my baby a piece of this dried
meat?" Running Alone asked Kaya. "She's getting a
new tooth, and she needs something to chew on."
She turned back to breaking strips of the meat and
putting the pieces into the mortar to be ground fine.

Kaya broke off a bit of the meat and held it to
Light On The Water's lips. But the baby pressed her
lips shut tightly, her eyes merry as if she and Kaya
were playing a game. "Isn't she precious!" Kaya

*Kaya kept Swan Circling in sight,
hoping to have a chance to talk with her again.*

exclaimed. Then she glanced at Swan Circling. Kautsa had said it was sad that she had no children yet. Did she mind that Kaya was making a fuss over the baby?

Swan Circling was using the large pestle. Her strong arms gleamed with sweat from the hard work. "When I saw you girls in the stream this morning, I thought of the time when I was your age," she said when Kaya caught her eye. "Do you like to swim?"

"Aa-heh!" Kaya said.

"So do I," Swan Circling said. "I come from a place where the Snake River joins the Big River. My friends and I swam every chance we got. My mother called us the Fish Girls. Someday I'll show you my favorite places to dive from the cliffs, Kaya."

"You're always thinking of the future, aren't you?" Eetsa said to Swan Circling. "Many times I've heard you say 'someday this' or 'someday that.'"

"It's true," Swan Circling said. She smiled at Eetsa, who was her good friend, and passed her the pestle. Then she wiped her face with the back of her hand. "Do you often think of what's to come, Kaya?"

Kaya was thinking that no one had ever asked her as many questions about herself as Swan Circling did. Kaya liked that. "I think of seeing my horse again," Kaya said. "Mostly I think of getting my little sister back. But I don't know how I can do that."

"When a way opens, you'll be ready," Swan Circling said with confidence. "I saw you riding with Two Hawks yesterday. I don't know how you persuaded him to get on a horse, but you did! He looked as if he was in a much better mood. You have a strong will, Kaya, and I'm glad you think of the needs of others."

Kaya gently rocked the baby in the tee-kas. Lulled by the motion and the voices of the women, Light On The Water was falling asleep. Oh, how Kaya wanted to be the girl Swan Circling believed her to be. And how she feared she wasn't!

"Pay attention, I have something to tell you," Kautsa said to Kaya and the other girls and women who were gathered around making baskets. On these long winter evenings, when the wind howled like a pack of wolves, they stayed close to the glowing fires in the warm lodge. Kautsa never missed a chance to teach the children with stories or legends. She was a wonderful storyteller and acted out the different parts with her hands and her low, musical voice.

Kautsa held up a basket made of cedar bark. "Here's a basket traded to me by one of our friends to the west," she said. "She told a story to go with the basket, a story about how Cedar Tree taught them basket making," she continued. "Listen, and I'll tell it to you."

Kaya sighed with pleasure. She glanced over her shoulder at Swan Circling, who was twining a basket as she listened with the others. Swan Circling caught Kaya's glance and nodded, as if to say, *Yes, I love to listen to stories, too.*

"It was so, my children, that a long time ago all the animals, plants, trees, and creatures could walk and talk the way that people do," Kautsa began. "In those long-ago days, Gray Squirrel was a girl, like all of you. But she was a little slow in her thoughts, and she was clumsy, too. Day after day she sat all alone under a cedar tree. Cedar Tree began to feel sorry for Gray Squirrel and decided to help her. He couldn't allow her to grow up without learning what a girl needs to know.

"Wise old Cedar Tree sent Gray Squirrel to pick beargrass, dry it, and put it into bundles. Then he told her where to find dyes and how to cut and dry his own roots to make cedar strips. When she had all the materials she needed to make a basket, he taught her how to weave it. She was so proud of her work! But Cedar Tree told her to dip her basket into the stream. Was it woven tightly enough to hold water? When water ran out of her basket, Gray Squirrel hung her head and cried.

"'Don't cry, little girl!' Cedar Tree said." Kautsa made her voice strong and low, the voice of a wise old tree. "He told her she'd have to practice and practice in order to make a basket successfully. Then he sent her out to look for designs to weave into her basket.

"Gray Squirrel went looking. Rattlesnake gave Gray Squirrel the zigzag design on his back. Mountain gave her the design of his peaks and valleys. Grouse gave her the design of his track marks. Stream gave her the design of his waves. To find all these designs, Gray Squirrel had studied the world so closely that now she was much, much wiser.

"Gray Squirrel wove a beautiful basket with all of the designs she'd been given. And when she dipped it into the Big River, her basket didn't leak! Now she was very proud of herself—and Cedar Tree was proud, too. But he told her that she should set down her basket in the woods and leave it there. She must give her basket back to the earth to show that she was thankful for what was given to her.

"Gray Squirrel didn't like that one bit! But Cedar Tree insisted that if she didn't give away the basket, she would never be a good weaver. And she had to make five little baskets and give away those, too! She must learn to work for others, not just for herself.

"Coyote was coming up the Big River at that time," Kautsa continued, finishing the story. "He saw Gray Squirrel's fine basket, and he was impressed with it. He told her that soon people would come into that part of the world. Already people were so close that Coyote could hear their footsteps. He said that from that day forward, the women of that land would be well known for their cedar baskets. And it's so, isn't it?" Kautsa spread her strong, gnarled hands on her knees.

One little girl gazed up at Kautsa longingly. "Tell us another story?" she asked.

Kautsa smiled. "Instead, why don't you make a little twined basket like the one Kaya is working on? I'll start it for you, and she'll help you if you get into trouble. Won't you, Granddaughter?"

"Aa-heh, Kautsa," Kaya said. She would do anything that her grandmother asked of her. But she hoped Swan Circling had heard how quickly she agreed to Kautsa's request—she wanted her friend to think well of her. It seemed that no matter what Kaya was doing, she had Swan Circling on her mind.

The next morning as Kaya stepped out of the stream where the girls had taken their morning swim, she saw Swan Circling beckoning to her. The frigid air made Kaya feel like running and jumping with energy. She pulled her elk robe around her and hurried to meet Swan Circling.

"Tawts may-we!" Kaya said.

"Aa-heh, tawts may-we, Kaya," Swan Circling said. "That story your grandmother told last night set me thinking. I have something I want to show you. Would you like to work with me today?"

"Aa-heh!" Kaya said. "If Kautsa says I may, I'll work with you."

"Run and ask her then," Swan Circling said. "I'll be in the lodge."

After Kautsa said that Kaya could work with Swan Circling, Kaya joined her again. Swan Circling was kneeling on a mat in the crowded lodge. Kaya knelt at her side and watched her untie the flaps of a large parfleche painted with triangle designs in red, blue, green, and yellow. "Your grandmother's story reminded me of a basket I made when I was a little girl—my very first one," Swan Circling said.

"My first was awfully lopsided," Kaya said, "but I gave it to Kautsa anyway."

Swan Circling lifted out her special ceremonial dress and moccasins from the parfleche and set them aside. Then she took out a little brown twined basket and handed it to Kaya. "You can see that my first basket's lopsided, too."

Kaya smiled at the lumpy little basket. She liked to imagine Swan Circling as a girl with small hands and big ideas—a girl just like Kaya. She was happy to be sitting at her friend's side. "Didn't you give your first basket to your grandmother?" she asked.

Swan Circling nodded. "Aa-heh, I did. After she died, it was given back to me. I'm glad. This basket taught me many lessons."

Kaya turned it over. With her fingertip she traced the weaving. "Was one of the lessons to make your twining tighter?"

Swan Circling smiled. "Aa-heh, to pull the cord tighter was one thing I learned. But that wasn't all— I learned about patience, too. I was a very bold, headstrong little girl. I thought that there was nothing I couldn't do!"

"But you can do everything, can't you?" Kaya asked.

Now Swan Circling laughed. "Of course I can't!" She put her warm hand on Kaya's knee. "You see, I'd been watching my grandmother weave her baskets, and I was sure I knew how. I decided I was going to make a beautiful one just like hers. I got my basket started, but I made mistake after mistake. Finally, I had this pitiful little thing to show her."

"What did she say about it?" Kaya asked.

"She thanked me and said I'd made a start. But I expected more praise than that," Swan Circling admitted. "I remember I was pouting. I asked her why she hadn't corrected my mistakes, as if the lumps in my basket were her fault! Then she told me, 'Everyone has to have her own experience. Everyone has to learn her own lessons.' Little by little I understood that to make a mistake is not a bad thing. But I should be wise enough not to make the same mistake again—and again."

Kaya understood that Swan Circling wasn't speaking now of basket making—she was speaking of life.

This was a chance for Kaya to tell Swan Circling about how she'd gotten her nickname and why the enemies were able to capture her and Speaking Rain—and about her guilt for escaping without her sister. She could tell Swan Circling the truth. "I've made mistakes, too," Kaya began. "I—"

Swan Circling waited for her to go on.

But then Kaya lost her nerve. What if she told Swan Circling the truth, but her friend lost respect for her? If she did, she wouldn't seek out Kaya anymore. No, Kaya couldn't risk losing Swan Circling's friendship.

"I left holes in a basket I was making," Kaya

said in a determined voice. "But my grandmother showed me right away so I could do a better job." She handed back the clumsy little basket.

Swan Circling repacked it with the other things and tied the parfleche. "Is something troubling you?" she asked Kaya. "There's a crease right here." She put her fingertip between Kaya's eyebrows.

Kaya didn't meet Swan Circling's gaze. "No, nothing's troubling me," she said.

Still Swan Circling waited. After a moment, she put the parfleche back on the stack against the lodge wall. "Maybe we've done enough talking," she said. "Come, let's pack up the pemmican and put it into storage."

A SICK BABY

During the night a light snow fell. Kaya was sweeping it away from the outside of the lodge when she heard a soft sound that gently rose and fell—the sound of a flute. She cocked her head. Someone was playing sweet, winding notes that sounded both happy and sad at the same time.

The melody made Kaya think of a warm spring breeze blowing in the depth of winter. Had Two Hawks finished the little flute she'd helped him begin? Was he playing it? When she'd swept the ground bare with the piece of sagebrush, she hurried to find him.

She found Two Hawks in the lodge near the

door. He was sitting with an older boy named Runs Home, who held a flute to his lips. The sweet music Kaya had heard was the older boy's skilled playing. Kaya knew Runs Home liked to serenade girls on long summer evenings.

When Two Hawks saw Kaya, he raised his flute to his lips and blew. A squeak! He blew again. Another shrill squeak and then a squawk!

Runs Home frowned. He took the flute from Two Hawks and compared it to his. He showed Two Hawks that the slit he'd made in the top was too small and the holes in the side were too large.

Two Hawks seized his flute and shoved it out of sight under a parfleche. He folded his arms over his chest and gave Kaya a fierce look of anger and disappointment.

Since Two Hawks had been with her people, he'd put on some weight and he looked much healthier, but at that moment he reminded her of the skinny, bitter boy she'd first seen in the enemy camp.

"Can you help him find another elderberry stick?" Runs Home asked her. "He can learn to make a good flute if he'll let me work with him."

Kaya threw Two Hawks the words, *Come with me. We'll find another stick.*

Two Hawks turned his head. Kaya thought that if his ankle was healed and he could run away from them, he would.

You can't make something perfect the first time you try, she signed to Two Hawks. *You have to practice! I'm going to get horses for us so we can find another stick for you.*

"Will he go with you?" Runs Home asked her.

"He did before," she said firmly. "He will again. I'm sure of it."

Listen to me, Runs Home signed to Two Hawks. *I'll teach you some things.*

Two Hawks looked closely at Runs Home, then at Kaya. He set his jaw and shrugged. Then he got to his feet and hobbled outside right at Kaya's heels, as if he was relieved that she and Runs Home hadn't let him quit on his first try.

Kaya and Brown Deer were helping Kautsa take wrapped camas cakes from a storage pit when a crier came riding through the village. "Friends are arriving! Get ready for them!" he called out. They

37

all stopped what they were doing and gathered to welcome their visitors.

A northeast wind, the coldest one, blew fine flakes of snow. Kaya shaded her eyes as she watched the horizon. Soon she saw a dark line of horses and riders come over the snow-covered rise and descend to the village.

What could be better in this cold season than the warmth of greeting friends and family! Everyone hugged and smiled and talked and handed around gifts. Men, women, and children crowded inside with their belongings until all the lodges were pleasantly full.

Kaya caught sight of Cut Cheek standing with *Toe-ta* and *Pi-lah-ka*. He'd come with the others from a winter village nearby. She'd forgotten how handsome Cut Cheek was, with his broad forehead, flashing eyes, and high cheekbones, a scar on one of them.

Would Brown Deer hurry to greet him, as others were doing? He was looking around the gathering. Kaya searched the crowd, too—where was her older sister?

Then Kaya saw her. Brown Deer was standing

modestly by the doorway of their lodge. Her cheeks were burning, as if she knew Cut Cheek was looking her way. Then she raised her eyes to his. Something passed between them like a shiver of heat lightning. Kaya smiled to herself and thought, *Someday soon Cut Cheek will wear the necklace Brown Deer is making!*

Kaya's aunt from a nearby village greeted her with a strong hug and a kiss. "Scouts told us about your capture and escape," she said. "We're so glad you're well!"

"Did your scouts have any news of my sister?" Kaya asked.

The smile left her aunt's face. "No one has any news of her," she said. "Of course, no one can cross the Buffalo Trail now. Our enemies must have taken her back to their country with them."

Biting her lip, Kaya turned away.

Swan Circling touched Kaya's arm. "Will you help me carry these baskets of food?" she asked Kaya gently. "We have so much to do for the gathering tonight."

When night came on, Kaya and the others dressed in their best clothes and entered the ceremonial lodge for the new year gathering. This was the shortest day of the year—and the darkest. The clouds had cleared, and stars shone in the sky, where the new moon, thin as a fish bone, had risen. Four big tepees had been put together to make this lodge, but soon the large space was crowded with people of all ages.

Several men held a drum made of hide. The fires in the center of the lodge cast their light on the walls, and the air smelled sweetly of cedar boughs and tule mats.

When everyone was in the lodge, To Soar Like An Eagle raised his hand to get attention. He wore a feathered headdress and a painted hide shirt decorated with porcupine quills. He was a very respected old chief with white eyebrows and a low, powerful voice that came from deep in his chest. Kaya watched his lined face as he spoke.

"Hun-ya-wat has made this night longer than all the others," To Soar Like An Eagle said. "In this darkest time, let us reflect on the days that have gone before and on the days that lie ahead. It is time to renew life."

The drummers began, filling the night with drumbeats that echoed back from the surrounding

hills. After the drumming, men and women began to speak of births and deaths and of the gifts Hun-ya-wat had given them in the past year. They told of good deeds and acts of bravery. They gave thanks for successful hunts and for ample fish and roots and berries. Together they prayed that all might keep their minds and hearts pure so there would be enough food in the year to come.

Kaya listened closely to the prayer songs. She looked at her parents and grandparents standing near her. Firelight played over their solemn faces. Brown Deer, too, was sober and thoughtful. Even the twins, such lively little boys, seemed to be listening closely to the singing.

Two Hawks, who couldn't understand the words, gazed steadily at the others as though he understood everything from their serious expressions.

Kaya could see Swan Circling standing with her young husband, Claw Necklace. Her dark eyes reflected the firelight, but her thoughts seemed far away, as if she was thinking of the future again.

Kaya considered her own life over the past year.

She had much to be thankful for, but she had many regrets, too. Her good and bad feelings mingled like the streams of smoke rising from the fires. Her eyes smarted with them.

When Kaya glanced again at Swan Circling, she realized what was troubling her most tonight—she hadn't yet told her friend how she got her nickname or how her disobedience had gotten her and Speaking Rain captured. She hadn't been brave enough. But until she did, Swan Circling wouldn't really know her.

Kaya closed her eyes. *Hun-ya-wat, make me honest and strong in character,* she prayed silently. *Help me face life with an honorable, truthful, and strong will.*

When the prayers came to an end, it was time for the midnight feast. Women brought out steaming salmon broth followed by bowls of mashed roots and

berries. As Kaya watched the preparations, she felt a quiet, calm resolve in her heart. Her prayer had given her courage. She would tell Swan Circling everything— and as soon as possible.

Kaya watched for a chance to speak with
Swan Circling, but with all the visitors crowded into
the lodges, they were never together. After several
days, the visitors left for their own villages. Now,
surely, Kaya could take Swan Circling aside and talk
with her.

One morning Kaya was piling wood beside the
cooking fires when Running Alone hurried over.
"Would you look after my baby for a little while?"
Running Alone asked Kaya. "I'm troubled about her.
I want to find Bear Blanket and ask her for help."

Kaya was worried as she followed Running
Alone through the lodge to her sleeping place. Bear
Blanket was a powerful medicine woman who had
cured many, many sick people. Light On The Water
must be sick, or Running Alone wouldn't be looking
for the medicine woman's help.

Light On The Water lay in a hide swing hung
from the lodge poles. Kaya leaned over her.
The baby's face was flushed, and each time
she drew a breath she coughed. Tiny beads
of sweat covered her forehead and cheeks.
Her eyes were open, but she didn't gaze up
at Kaya. She didn't seem to see anything at all.

When Running Alone hurried off, Kaya placed her finger in the baby's hot little hand. Light On The Water didn't tug at it, as she usually did. "Are you sick, little one?" Kaya whispered. "There's help for you. You won't be sick for long."

Soon Bear Blanket came through the door of the lodge. She was an old, gray-haired woman, but her back was as straight as an arrow. Kaya knew that Bear Blanket always kept her mind and body clean so she would be ready to help those who needed her. Her animal spirit helper was a grizzly bear. Long ago she had received medicine power—the power to heal—from this *wyakin*.

Bear Blanket carried a medicine bundle in one hand. Swan Circling followed right behind her.

Running Alone motioned for Kaya to stand aside so that Bear Blanket could see the baby. The old woman studied the baby's face and bent over to listen to her coughing. Then she spread her hands over the baby's head and began to sing one of her medicine songs.

As she sang, she passed her hands up and down over Light On The Water's body. Kaya saw the baby's eyelids tremble and shut, then open

44

*The old woman studied the baby's face
and bent over to listen to her coughing.*

again when she coughed harder.

Bear Blanket drew Swan Circling aside and spoke to her, then went back to her singing.

Swan Circling frowned. "She wants me to bring her the inner bark of a special tree to boil for a healing drink," she said to Running Alone. "I'm going to get my horse and go after it now."

"But it's very cold," Running Alone said. "The northeast wind is blowing again. Will you be all right?"

"I can't wait," Swan Circling said. "Your baby needs the medicine now."

Running Alone put her hand on Swan Circling's arm. "Then hurry!" she urged her. "Kaya will round up your horse for you while you get your blankets and your knife."

Kaya threw a deerskin over her shoulders and grabbed a rope bridle. Her breath was a white plume at her lips as she ran out to the herd grazing near the village. She found Swan Circling's white-faced horse, placed the bridle on her lower jaw, and rode her back to the lodges.

Swan Circling was wearing otter-skin leggings and mittens and had her elk robe around her. She

held her beautiful saddle of wood and painted rawhide. Kaya reined in the horse and slipped off. She put on the saddle and reached under the horse's belly for the cinch. Already Swan Circling was hanging her bags from the saddle horn.

"Cinch it snugly," Swan Circling told her. "I'm going to ride as fast as possible. Bear Blanket said the baby is very sick." She tested the saddle cinch with her weight, then swung up. "Good work, Kaya. I'll be back before last light. Watch for me." She urged her horse forward and, in a few strides, was running full out across the frozen ground.

"I'll watch for you!" Kaya called after her. But the wind snatched away her words.

All day Kaya stayed with Running Alone and her baby. Bear Blanket sang her medicine songs, but the baby only coughed harder and harder. Her little face was red, and her eyes screwed shut with her effort to breathe. Kaya watched her anxiously—did the baby have the terrible sickness of blisters that the men with pale faces had brought to the land? Kaya was afraid to ask.

As the light began to fade, Kaya went to watch for Swan Circling's return. At dusk there were no colors in the valley. The river was a shining black curve, like a snake, and the trees were black slashes against the white snow. Under dark clouds, a hawk rode the wind in slow, wide turns.

Where is Swan Circling? Kaya thought. *Why doesn't she come back?*

Then she saw a horse appear in the trees at the far end of the valley. Kaya ran up the hillside a little way to get a better look. The horse had a white face—Swan Circling's horse. Kaya caught her breath in relief. But as the horse came closer, out of the trees, Kaya saw that it was limping as though it was hurt—and that it had no rider.

GIFTS FROM
SWAN CIRCLING

Kaya watched as Claw Necklace, Toe-ta, and two other men saddled their horses and rode off to search for Swan Circling. Kaya couldn't believe that anything bad could have happened to her friend—she was so young, so strong. Maybe she'd fallen off her horse, and it had run away from her. Surely she was coming home on foot and the men would soon meet up with her. In the meantime, here was her bag—still hanging on the saddle horn.

Kaya ran with the bag to find Bear Blanket. The medicine woman was with Running Alone and her baby, who lay gasping in the baby swing. Bear Blanket opened the bag and took out a handful of bark. "This is the good medicine I asked for," she said.

"Tawts!" Running Alone exclaimed. "I knew Swan Circling wouldn't fail us."

Kaya dug her fingernails into her palms as she gazed down at the baby's red face and dry lips. Would blisters soon break out on her cheeks? Her people had never seen the men with pale faces, but their sicknesses had killed many Nimíipuu. "Tell me," she asked fearfully, "does the baby have the bad sickness that kills?"

"Not that," Bear Blanket said quickly. "She has a weakness in her chest."

Kaya unclenched her fists. "Will the medicine help her, then?"

"I'll make a healing drink with it," Bear Blanket said. "Soon she'll breathe more easily. Go rest, Kaya. There's nothing you can do now."

Kaya was warm under a blanket of woven strips of rabbit fur, but she couldn't sleep. Her thoughts were with Swan Circling, who was somewhere in the darkness and the cold wind. Perhaps she'd built herself a lean-to for shelter, as Kaya had done when she escaped from the enemies. Or maybe, any moment now, Swan Circling would come walking into the lodge with Claw Necklace. She had to be all right!

Kaya slept fitfully. Before first light she awoke to a cold draft on her cheek. She pushed up onto her elbow. A few people were stirring in the lodge, and someone had pulled back the covering of the doorway. Had Swan Circling returned? Kaya crawled from underneath her blanket. She saw Eetsa leaving the lodge, a torch in her hand. Kaya pulled her elk hide robe around her shoulders, followed Eetsa to the door, and peeked out.

The moon had already set, and the sky was turning gray. In the space between the lodges, Eetsa joined a group of men and women. Kaya saw Kautsa, Pi-lah-ka, and other elders wrapped in their robes. Toe-ta was speaking to them. And now she made out Claw Necklace walking toward the lodges. He carried something. Kaya blinked. Then she realized it was Swan Circling that Claw Necklace held in his arms.

Kaya couldn't get her breath. No!—Swan Circling would be all right! She would be! Kaya pulled her robe over her head and hid her face in it.

In a moment she felt firm hands on her shoulders. She lifted her chin and looked up into Kautsa's face. In the gray early light, her grandmother looked very old and very tired. "Our men found her body beside the stream," Kautsa said quietly. "It seems her horse broke through thin ice and stumbled, and she was thrown off. Her head struck a boulder, and the blow killed her." She opened her arms and took Kaya into her warm embrace.

Through her tears, Kaya heard Kautsa's gentle voice at her ear. "She was full of light and love," Kautsa said. "It's hard to let her go, but we must help her spirit journey on."

Kaya walked in a daze after Swan Circling's death. She felt as if a jagged hole had been torn in her heart. Mixed in with the pain of her friend's death was another pain—one of regret. Oh, why hadn't she quickly called up the courage to tell Swan Circling everything? Now it was too late.

Everyone in the village grieved and mourned for Swan Circling. They comforted each other with gentle words and tried to console Claw Necklace, too. Runners took the bad news to neighboring villages. Though it was the heart of winter, one runner volunteered to travel all the way to the Big River to tell Swan Circling's family.

None of Swan Circling's family lived close enough to help with the burial, so the women in her husband's family took charge of all the preparations. They got to work right away. The best hide workers took out fresh white deer hides, clean and unused, to make a new dress and moccasins to clothe the body. Other women prepared food to serve the whole community after the burial ceremony. Some stayed with the body, never leaving it alone, even for a moment.

Kaya stayed close to Running Alone and her baby. The medicine had helped Light On The Water. She wasn't coughing so hard now, and she gazed up at Kaya's face when Kaya rocked the sling and sang to her. Light On The Water didn't need encouragement to sleep, though—she was still weak and listless.

Even when the baby slept, Kaya kept singing the lullaby, "She's the precious one, my own dear little precious one." She was sure Swan Circling was listening. Until her body was buried, her spirit would stay close by.

Kaya was gently rocking the sleeping baby when she thought she heard a canyon wren singing somewhere near the lodge. Kaya cocked her head. Was Swan Circling sending a message through a bird? Kaya went outside to look for it.

Wrapped in his antelope hide, Two Hawks was standing near the lodge. He still used a stick for a crutch, but he could put more weight on his leg now. He saw Kaya and limped over to meet her. When he was in front of her, he put the little flute he'd been working on to his lips. His cheeks puffed out as he played *tee, tee*— the sweet, descending notes she'd mistaken for birdsong.

"That's a pretty sound," Kaya said. "May I look at your flute?"

He handed it over. His face was solemn, but his dark eyes were lively—she saw that he was proud of what he'd made.

The little flute had a good feel in her hands. It was well and carefully made, and Two Hawks had smoothed the wood to a gloss. "Tawts!" she said. "Good work, Two Hawks."

"Runs Home helped me," he said. "He's my friend now."

"I see he's helping you with words, too," she said. "And you've made a good flute. Now you have to learn to play it."

"I can play!" he insisted. He brought the flute to his lips and blew, his eyes narrowed in concentration. *Tee, tee, tew,* he played. This time he was able to add a third note to the song.

Two Hawks's success lifted Kaya's sad heart a little. His leg was healing, and he was a happier boy now. And it seemed that Light On The Water would get well. These were things to be thankful for in this dark time. Surely Swan Circling's spirit would find comfort in these things, too.

Before first light on the third morning after Swan Circling's death, Toe-ta and other men went to the burial place on a rise above the stream to dig a grave. When they sent word that the grave was ready, everyone gathered in the faint light for the ceremony.

Swan Circling's body and some of her things

had been wrapped in clean hides and fresh mats and placed on a horse-drawn travois. Fighting her tears, Kaya followed with the others as the body was taken to the burial place—which faced the east, where the sky would soon brighten.

A medicine man with strong spirit powers led the way. He was a short man with a broad chest and shoulders, and he wore a fur headdress set with mountain sheep horns. At the graveside, he praised Swan Circling's strength, her unwavering courage, and her willingness to help her people. He spoke of everyone's sorrow to lose such a good woman. Then he urged her spirit to travel on.

As the first streak of dawn stained the pale sky, the men placed the body in the shallow grave and covered it with another mat. First the women, then the men stepped one by one to the grave and dropped in a handful of earth. When it was Kaya's turn, she vowed silently, *All my life I'll think of you! I'll strive to be like you, I promise!*

But Swan Circling's spirit wouldn't be able to rest until all of her belongings had been given away or burned. Because Eetsa had been a close friend of

Swan Circling, she took charge of the give-away.

In the lodge, Eetsa placed all of Swan Circling's belongings on a mat. After all the people had eaten the meal the women had prepared, they gathered around the mat. One by one, Toe-ta called them to step forward. With a few words, he gave Running Alone the mortar and pestle. Little Fawn received the digging stick, and Kautsa a large parfleche. To Brown Deer he gave a pair of deerskin moccasins. He gave other women and girls Swan Circling's baskets, necklaces, shells, and hides until there was nothing left on the mat by his feet but Swan Circling's saddle.

Then Toe-ta motioned for Kaya to come forward. She kept her gaze on her moccasins as her father spoke to her. "Claw Necklace told me his wife admired your care for horses and your love of them," he said gently. "He's certain she would want you to have her saddle."

"Katsee-yow-yow," Kaya murmured.

Then Toe-ta rubbed his lips with his thumb. He thought a moment. "She also wanted you to have something much more important than a saddle," he said.

In his deep voice Toe-ta told how Swan Circling
had recently come to him and Eetsa and asked
to speak with them. "She told us she had a dark
dream, a dream of her death," he said. "She wasn't
frightened, but she said that if she should die, she
wanted Kaya to have her name. As you know, her
name was hers to give as she chose. She was fond
of you, Kaya, and she spoke of your special friendship. She believed you would carry her name well.
We accepted her gift to you with gratitude."

Now a very old woman lifted her head to speak.
It was her job to remember how everyone was
related to each other. "What Kaya's father says is
true," she said firmly. "I was there when Kaya's
parents accepted the name. I say this is so."

Kaya hugged the beautiful saddle of painted
wood and hide that Toe-ta had handed her. But as
she turned and walked back to her place, her mind
couldn't take in the second gift that Swan Circling
had given. Her name! That was the greatest gift
anyone could give. Kaya's thoughts rushed back
and forth between gratitude and doubt. How
honored she was to have been given her friend's
name! But could she truly be worthy of it? And

*"She also wanted you to have something
much more important than a saddle," he said.*

would Swan Circling have given it if she'd known Kaya's failures? If only Swan Circling were here, for it seemed to Kaya that her friend was the one person who could quiet these racing doubts and fears. But Kaya was alone with her torn feelings.

It wasn't until that night that Kaya could talk with her mother. Eetsa had heated stones in the fire and was putting them into a water basket to boil deer meat. She stirred the hot stones rapidly to keep them from scorching the basket. Kaya crouched by her side.

"Eetsa, I'm troubled about my namesake," Kaya said, careful not to say the name of the dead out loud.

Eetsa lifted out the cooled stones with a forked stick and put in more hot ones. "What troubles you, Daughter?" she asked.

"I don't think she'd have given me her name if she'd known the mistakes I've made," Kaya admitted. "I never told her about my nickname or how I got myself and Speaking Rain taken captive."

When Eetsa glanced at her, Kaya saw her mother's eyes soften. "But there's nothing to be troubled about," Eetsa said. "She knew about your nickname, but she said it didn't matter to her. And she said it took great strength to leave your sister behind and that you were wise to do so."

"She said that to you?" Kaya asked.

"Aa-heh," Eetsa assured her. "She often spoke about you. She told me she had confidence that you would grow to be trustworthy and strong. And she said you have a generous heart, Daughter—which you do. It's not time for you to use her name yet, but when that time comes, you'll know. Is anything else troubling you?"

Kaya pressed her lips together and shook her head. Her heart was full—she was afraid that if she spoke, she'd burst into tears of both gratitude and relief.

The next morning, Kaya sat with her little brothers on her rabbit-fur blanket. The twins lay on their stomachs with their chins in their hands. They were watching as she shaped and tied long pine needles to make three little horses.

"Is one of those horses for me?" Wing Feather asked.

"If my brother gets a toy, so do I!" Sparrow demanded. "Don't I, Kaya?"

"Yes, one of these horses is for you," she said, tapping Wing Feather on his nose. "And one's for you," she told Sparrow and tugged his braid.

Kaya put the finishing touches on the little horses and handed one to each boy. "Here they are," she said. "Now you can have races."

"Katsee-yow-yow!" the twins said at the same time. They seized their toys and scampered with them to the pile of hides where other children were playing.

Kaya cut a small piece of hide and tied it with a bit of fringe onto the third little horse's back—there, now this one had a saddle. Then she wrapped herself in her elk robe and left the lodge without telling anyone where she was going. Since she'd wakened, she'd known what she must do.

The trail to the burial place led around the sides of low hills. Bare trees cast blue shadows on the thin covering of snow. Coyotes hunting rabbits had left tracks in the snow, and she saw the wing print of a hawk that had swooped down for a kill.

On the east-facing side of the hill, she turned off the trail. There were many graves here, marked with rocks. Mourners had left small gifts on some of them. Kaya went to the place Swan Circling was buried and put the little horse made of pine needles on her grave.

"I've been thinking about things," Kaya said softly to her friend. "I want you to know I'm going to live up to your expectations—and that I'm grateful for your trust. And your name. But I hope to get my sister back before I use it, and maybe my horse, too. I want to deserve what you've given me. I want our people to think well of me when they call me by your name."

Kaya looked back at her village. In the cold, only dogs moved between the lodges. Everything was quiet, but soon family and friends would return for the Winter Spirit Dances, and the village would be crowded again. She stood a moment more, squinting into the morning light that flooded the long, broad valley, and then she started home.

Looking
Back
1764

A PEEK INTO
THE PAST

*Painted hide bags called **parfleches** (par-fleshes) held dried food for winter.*

By *sek-le-wahl*, the time when trees drop their leaves and cold and snow come to the high country, most traveling, trading, fishing, and food gathering slowed down. It was a quiet time for being inside, warm and close with family and friends, while rivers froze and thick snow blanketed the land.

In winter, there was plenty of time for making and mending all the beautiful, useful clothing and tools Nez Perces needed all year round. Men and boys made ropes from horsehair, wove hemp into nets for fishing, whittled sticks to make arrows, and chipped stones to make sharp arrowheads. They glued feathers to the ends of their arrows to help them fly swift and straight.

Girls and women twined the fibers of beargrass and hemp into cord, and then wove the cord into bags and hats. They used berry or root stains to create beautiful patterns. With sharp bone needles and thread of sinews, they stitched animal hides into new moccasins, shirts, leggings, and dresses for their families. It took two deer hides to make one dress, and Nez Perce women often kept a deer's tail as a decorative detail on the front of their dresses. Clothing was also adorned with shells, beads, and colored porcupine quills. Girls and women softened the quills by soaking them. Then they flattened the quills and sewed them onto animal hides.

Elk teeth were the most prized adornments of all. Only the two front teeth of an elk were used to decorate clothing. If a woman or girl had many elk teeth sewn on her dress, it meant she had a powerful hunter in her family!

Buffalo bladder pouch for storing porcupine quills

Elk teeth, long white dentalium shells, and lots of beads decorate this dress from the 1850s. In Kaya's time, there weren't so many beads, but the same designs could be made with porcupine quills.

67

This contemporary Nez Perce girl has fur wrapped around her braids, a style worn in Kaya's time, too.

During the winter months, most Nez Perce men, women, and children wore warm clothes made out of thicker hides and wrapped warm robes around their shoulders. They also wore fur moccasins, leggings, mittens, and capes, and they tied pieces of fur around their necks.

The Nez Perces saved much of the dried roots, berries, fish, and meat that they gathered in the warm months for winter. The village's store of food was shared by all families, regardless of who had done the hunting or gathering. If the hunts had been successful and the harvests plentiful, the food would last the village until spring. It was rare that villages ran short of food. If they did, men sometimes went out on snowshoes to hunt deer or elk, and women searched out nourishing mosses to roast.

Winter villages were nestled along rivers and streams in valleys beneath high hills that provided protection from the wind and snow.

Snowshoes helped Nez Perces hunt more easily when snows were deep.

A hunting party returns to a lodge where women are preparing a meal.

Several families lived together for warmth, company, and protection in large homes made of a framework of lodge poles covered with mats of reeds and grasses. These lodges, or "longhouses," could be up to 200 feet or longer. Fires burned in a row down the middle of the lodge, and two families shared each fire. They piled their belongings and slept on soft mattresses of dried grasses and bark along the outside walls. Smoke escaped and daylight entered through holes in the roof. In the dusky and crowded interior of the lodge, men, women, and children cooked, slept, talked and told stories, and went about their daily work.

But the winter months weren't all about hard work and lean times. They were also an important time for ceremonies.

Nez Perces held one of their most important ceremonies—the medicine dances, or *way-yak-wee-tset*—in the winter. For days or even a week at a time, family and friends gathered in a longhouse for all-night ceremonial dancing and to sing the songs taught to them by their guardian spirits. The Nez Perce believed that spirits, who usually took the form of animals or birds, granted people special powers and helped them throughout their lives. Children Kaya's age were permitted to watch the dances because one day, after their guardian spirit came to them during their vision quest, they, too, would take part in the dancing.

Best of all, on cold winter nights, children gathered to listen to their elders tell stories and legends, often about how the animals lived before humans came. Some stories explained how certain landmarks came to be. And some were just for fun. Children like Kaya learned them all by heart. In time, they would tell them to their own children and grandchildren. Nez Perces still share these stories today. Perhaps this winter a young Nez Perce girl is listening to this legend about sharing food, an especially important lesson during wintertime.

Elders mended or wove or whittled as they told stories and legends.

70

The Glutton

A husband and wife lived together, away from many people. Each day the woman dug roots for them to eat. Each day the man went hunting, but brought back nothing.

One day the woman thought, "I will hide today and find out why he never shoots anything." She saw the man shoot a grouse, and then another, and another. That night, the woman waited for him to tell her about the grouse, but he said nothing.

The next day the woman hid and waited until the man left. She found where he had thrown all the feathers and bones. *He has been cheating me!* the woman thought. Then she packed up and went away.

When the man came home, he saw feathers and bones strewn about. *She has found me out*, he thought. He decided to go to where the people were gathered and look for her.

The people were making merry, and the woman was dancing and surrounded by men. The husband became very angry. He took an arrow, drew back his bow, and aimed at her. She turned to him and said, "It does not happen to be that I am a grouse." Her talk made him feel ashamed. He dropped his bow and went straight home. The woman stayed right there.

GLOSSARY OF NEZ PERCE WORDS

In the story, Nez Perce words are spelled so that English readers can pronounce them. Here, you can also see how the words are actually spelled and said by the Nez Perce people.

Phonetic/Nez Perce	Pronunciation	Meaning
aa-heh/'éehe	*AA-heh*	yes, that's right
Eetsa/Iice	*EET-sah*	Mother
Hun-ya-wat/ Hanyaw'áat	*hun-yah-WAHT*	the Creator
katsee-yow-yow/ qe'ci'yew'yew'	*KAHT-see-yow-yow*	thank you
Kautsa/Qaaca'c	*KOUT-sah*	grandmother from mother's side
Kaya'aton'my'	*ky-YAAH-ton-my*	she who arranges rocks
Nimíipuu	*Nee-MEE-poo*	The People; known today as the Nez Perce Indians
Pi-lah-ka/piláqá	*pee-LAH-kah*	grandfather from mother's side
Salish/Sélix	*SAY-leesh*	friends of the Nez Perce who live near them
sek-le-wáal/ sexliwetés	*sehk-le-WAHL*	the time when trees drop their leaves and cold and snow come to the high country
tawts/ta'c	*TAWTS*	good

72

tawts may-we/ ta'c méeywi	*TAWTS MAY-wee*	good morning
tee-kas/tikée's	*tee-KAHS*	baby board, or cradleboard
Toe-ta/Toota'a	*TOH-tah*	Father
wah-tu/weet'u	*wah-TOO*	no
way-yak-wee-tset/ wéeyekweecet	*WAY-yak-wee-tset*	winter medicine dances
wyakin/ wéeyekin	*WHY-ah-kin*	guardian spirit

THE BOOKS ABOUT KAYA

MEET KAYA • An American Girl
Kaya's boasting gets her into big trouble
and earns her a terrible nickname.

KAYA'S ESCAPE! • A Survival Story
Kaya and her sister, Speaking Rain, are captured in
an enemy raid. Can they find a way to escape?

KAYA'S HERO • A Story of Giving
Kaya becomes close friends with a warrior
woman named Swan Circling, who inspires
Kaya and gives her an amazing gift.

KAYA AND LONE DOG • A Friendship Story
Kaya befriends a lone dog, who teaches her
about love and letting go.

KAYA SHOWS THE WAY • A Sister Story
Kaya is reunited with Speaking Rain, who has
a surprising decision to share.

CHANGES FOR KAYA • A Story of Courage
Kaya and her horse, Steps High, are caught
in a flash fire. Can they outrun it?

Coming in Spring 2003
WELCOME TO KAYA'S WORLD • 1764
History is lavishly illustrated with
photographs, illustrations, and artifacts
of the Nez Perce people.

MORE TO DISCOVER!

While books are the heart of The American Girls Collection, they are only the beginning. The stories in the Collection come to life when you act them out with the beautiful American Girls dolls and their exquisite clothes and accessories. To request a free catalogue full of things girls love, send in this postcard, call **1-800-845-0005,** or visit our Web site at **americangirl.com**.

Please send me an American Girl® catalogue.

My name is _____

My address is _____

City _____ State _____ Zip _____

My birth date is ___/___/___ E-mail address _____
           month day year   Fill in to receive updates and web-exclusive offers.

                                                                        12583i

Parent's signature _____

And send a catalogue to my friend.

My friend's name is _____

Address _____

City _____ State _____ Zip _____

                                                                           12591i

If the postcard has already been removed from this book
and you would like to receive an American Girl® catalogue,
please send your name and address to:

American Girl
P.O. Box 620497
Middleton, WI 53562-0497

You may also call our toll-free number, **1-800-845-0005,**
or visit our Web site at **americangirl.com**.

Place
Stamp
Here

PO BOX 620497
MIDDLETON WI 53562-0497

J

(American girls collection)